When Lions Roar

When

Lions Roar

by Robie H. Harris   pictures by Chris Raschka

ORCHARD BOOKS • NEW YORK • AN IMPRINT OF SCHOLASTIC INC.

For Hilary, Emily, David, and Ben—with love—R.H.H.
For Wendell Arneson, my teacher—C.R.

Text copyright © 2013 by Robie Harris
Illustrations copyright © 2013 by Chris Raschka

Library of Congress Cataloging-in-Publication Data
Harris, Robie H.
When lions roar / by Robie H. Harris : illustrated by Chris Raschka.   p. cm.
Summary: Loud, scary noises frighten a child until quiet and calmness return.
ISBN 978-0-545-11283-3
1. Noise—Juvenile fiction. 2. Fear—Juvenile fiction.
3. Emotions—Juvenile fiction. [1. Noise—Fiction. 2. Fear—Fiction.
3. Emotions—Fiction.] I. Raschka, Christopher, ill. II. Title.
PZ7.H2436Whe 2013   813.54—dc23   2012005622

10 9 8 7 6 5 4 3 2   16 17

Printed in China   38
First printing, October 2013

The illustrations are crayon and watercolor.
Book design by David Saylor and Charles Kreloff

When lions roar!

When monkeys screech!

When lightning cracks!

When thunder booms!

When sirens blare!

When big dogs bark!

When daddies yell!

When mommies holler!

The scary is near!

The scary is here!

So I sit right down.

Shut my eyes tight.

"Go away," I say.

"Scary! Go away."

And then–

the quiet is back.

So I open my eyes.

I stand right up.

The wind is still.

The sun is out.

A flower blooms.

An ant crawls by.

A puppy snoozes.

A kid swings high.

A mommy sings...

A daddy dances . . .

The scary is gone.

And I go on my way.

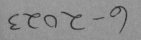